Ricky Ricotta's Mighty Robot
ASTRO-ACTIVITY
BOOK O' FUN

W9-ATN-441

by DAV PILKEY
pictures by MARTIN ONTIVEROS

THE BLUE SKY PRESS • AN IMPRINT OF SCHOLASTIC INC. • NEW YORK

THE BLUE SKY PRESS

ISBN-13: 978-0-439-82601-3
ISBN-10: 0-439-82601-2

12 11 10 9 8 7 6 5 4 3   10 11 12 13 14/0
Printed in the United States of America   40

First printing, March 2006

Contents

Hello, everybody! I'm Ricky Ricotta, and this is my Mighty Robot. We're blasting off for a trip across the solar system, with plenty of stops for fun and games along the way!

First, we need an easy way to remember the order of the planets: **M**ercury, **V**enus, **E**arth, **M**ars, **J**upiter, **S**aturn, **U**ranus, **N**eptune, **P**luto.

We made up this silly sentence to help us:

My **V**ery **E**normous **M**other **J**ust **S**wallowed **U**p **N**ine **P**izzas.

If you don't want to offend your mother, you can make up your own silly sentence below:

My **V**ery

Evil **M**ob

Just **S**wallowed

Up **N**eptune

Poop.

MERCURY

I'm Mr. Mosquito.

My meals melt into

mush on Mercury,

and it makes me

mighty mad!

TRUE-OR-FALSE FACTS
Which facts are fake? Circle true or false.

1. Mercury is the second smallest planet in our solar system. **TRUE** FALSE

2. Mercury gets very hot (up to 800 degrees) because it is the closest planet to the sun. **TRUE** FALSE

3. The dark side of Mercury gets very, very cold (as low as 300 degrees below zero). **TRUE** FALSE

4. Mercury is made up of molten rock, sulphuric acid, tin foil, and rubber bands.
TRUE FALSE

5. Mercury was named after the Roman god of commerce, travel, and thievery. **TRUE FALSE**

6. Like the moon, Mercury is covered with craters.
TRUE FALSE

7. Mercury's gravity is weaker than Earth's. If you weigh 85 pounds on Earth, you'll weigh about 32 pounds on Mercury.
TRUE FALSE

8. Because of this, Mercury has become a popular vacation destination for fat people.
TRUE FALSE

Evil Escape Maze

SQUEAKYVILLE JAIL

Mutant Mosquito Mumble-Jumble

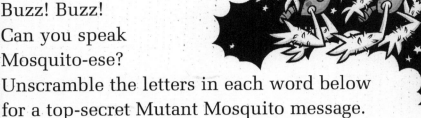

Buzz! Buzz!
Can you speak
Mosquito-ese?
Unscramble the letters in each word below
for a top-secret Mutant Mosquito message.

S Y M S E   D T E E L M

_ _ _ _ _   _ _ _ _ _ _

K M L I   E A L O C T H C O

_ _ _ _   _ _ _ _ _ _ _ _ _

S K E M A   S E M O O S Q T U I

_ _ _ _ _   _Mosquito_ _

D M A !

_ _ _ !

✳ EXTRA-TERRESTRIAL TIP ✳
K I R Y C = <u>R I C K Y</u>

9

Q. Why didn't Mr. Mosquito get burned when he visited the sun?
A. Because he went at night.

Q. What do naughty night crawlers sing?
A. Neptunes!

Q. What do you get when the Mighty Robot sneezes?
A. Out of the way!

Q. What is Major Monkey's favorite snack?
A. Mars-mallows.

Q. How does Uncle Unicorn hold up his pants?
A. With an asteroid belt.

Q. When does Dr. Stinky eat lunch?
A. At launch time.

Q. Which candy bars do you eat on Venus?
A. Melty Ways.

LAFFS AND JOKES

Q. What's worse than finding a Uranium Unicorn in your bedroom?
A. Finding two.

Q. What's a Stupid Stinkbug's favorite meal?
A. Stench fries.

Q. What did they name the world's sorriest spaceship?
A. The Apollo G.

Q. Which planet is purple and has seeds?
A. The Planet of the Grapes.

Ricky: Mom, can I go out and watch the eclipse of the sun?
Mom: Yes, dear, but don't stand too close.

Q. How did the Lunar Lambs get to the moon?
A. In a rocket sheep.

Q. How do we know that Saturn was married more than once?
A. Because it has a lot of rings.

Fun in the Sun

Which facts are fake? Circle true or false.

1. Deep inside the sun, hydrogen gas is heated to 27 million degrees. **TRUE** FALSE

2. The sun is so big, it could hold more than a million Earths. **TRUE** FALSE

3. The sun cools down at night to a temperature of just under 64 degrees. **TRUE** FALSE

4. Violent explosions of hot gases called solar flares erupt on the sun's surface and can be thousands of miles high. **TRUE** FALSE

5. People who live on the sun are called "Sunyuns." **TRUE** FALSE

6. The sun is a star, not a planet. **TRUE** FALSE

7. The sun is 93 million miles away from Earth, and it takes 8 minutes for the sun's light to reach here. **TRUE** FALSE

HOW TO DRAW A MECHA-MOSQUITO

1.

2.

3.

4.

5.

6.

7.

8.

9.

10.

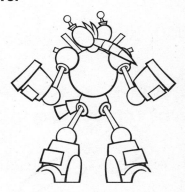

11.

12.

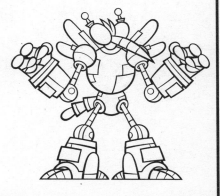

VENUS

Victor Von Vulture
is very vicious.
Don't ask "vy"
or he'll voodoo
you, too!

TRUE-OR-FALSE FACTS
Which facts are fake? Circle true or false.

1. Venus is hotter than the planet Mercury, even though it is farther from the sun. **TRUE FALSE**

2. The cloud cover on Venus traps heat from the sun and really makes things sizzle—up to 900 degrees. **TRUE FALSE**

3. It takes 243 Earth days to make one day on Venus. **TRUE FALSE**

4. Venus is covered with clouds that contain poisonous sulphuric acid. **TRUE** FALSE

5. The surface of Venus is made of rich milk chocolate. The core is believed to be composed of peanut-butter nougat and chewy caramel.
TRUE **FALSE**

6. Venus was discovered by the Greeks, who called it Bananarama. **TRUE** FALSE

7. Venus is called Earth's sister planet because it is similar in size and mass to Earth.
TRUE FALSE

8. Venus has more than 400 volcanoes that are at least 12 miles in diameter and thousands of smaller ones. **TRUE** FALSE

9. Venus can be seen from Earth with a naked eye. But it cannot be seen with a fully clothed eye.
TRUE FALSE

Victor Von Vulture just sent a new command to
his pesky pals on Venus. Use the key below
to help Ricky and his Robot decode
Victor's message before it's too late!

A	B	C	D	E	F	G	H	I
☺	●	$	→	✳	?	◆	<	∞

J	K	L	M	N	O	P	Q	R
¢	=	♥	÷	#	◗	@	▲	□

S	T	U	V	W	X	Y	Z
☉	▼	>	■	+	☹	★	%

z a p   a l l   t h e
% ☺ @   ☺ ♥ ♥   ▼ < ✳

c h e e s e   i n
$ < ✳ ✳ ⊙ ✳   ∞ #

s q u e a k y v i l l e
⊙ ▲ > ✳ ☺ = ★ ■ ∞ ♥ ♥ ✳

w i t h   u t t r a - l v i t
+ ∞ ▼ <   > ♥ ▼ □ ☺   ✳ ■ ∞ ▼

v o o d o
■ ◗ ◖ → ◗ ◗

r a y s   s o
□ ☺ ★ ⊙   ⊙ ◗

w e   c a n
+ ✳ $ ☺ #

t a k e   o v e r
▼ ☺ = ✳   ◗ ■ ✳ □

e a r t h !
✳ ☺ □ ▼ <

Verbal Vortex

A gas cloud on Venus has created quite a rage
and jumbled all the words hidden on this page.
Look for the words below in the puzzle
on the right. Look across, down,
and diagonally.

Asteroid	Neptune
Earth	Pluto
Galaxy	Saturn
Jupiter	Squeakyville
Mars	Star
Mercury	Sun
Meteor	Universe
Milky Way	Uranus
Moon	Venus

```
C A S E H W K U G A L A X Y E
O M P Q P E N D N B Z Y P V N
D I V A U I A E I I O H I E O
T L M E T E O R P D V M Y N P
K K X S S P A W T X A E B U A
O Y O H T C S K P F M A R S S
S W A M A N T I Y A S R I S T
T A J S R A R E R V L T J P E
A Y T U T K O T M A I H U I R
M Q T N P R D U E O M L P F O
U A U L Z I O N R W O I L O I
S L U P L U T O C A V N L E D
P V E N U M N E U J N A O K R
O N E P T U N E R O Z U X V A
J K M O O P H A Y B M I S U M
```

ROBOT RIDE
Coloring Page

B U I L D - A - B O T

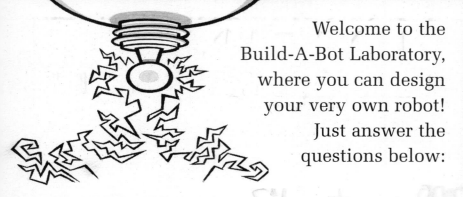

Welcome to the
Build-A-Bot Laboratory,
where you can design
your very own robot!
Just answer the
questions below:

What is your robot's name? _Sibertrong___

What is it made of? _medle_____

How tall is it? _2 feet_____

Can it fly? _yes_____

What special Robo-Powers does it have?

_cleaning, flying,_____

_battleing)_____

What cool equipment does it have?

_~~wm~~ micbles, jetpack_____

_sweeper_____

!!! IT'S ALIVE !!!

DR. _____Corbin_____ INVENTS ROBOT
(your name)

(draw a picture of your robot above)

EARTH

My Robot and I

like to roam,

but our favorite

planet is home,

sweet home.

TRUE-OR-FALSE FACTS
Which facts are fake? Circle true or false.

1. The surface of Earth is made of soil and rock.
TRUE FALSE

2. Beneath the surface is a ball of rock and metal, made of layers. The center layer—the inner core—is a ball of solid metal that may be as hot as 12,000 degrees. **TRUE FALSE**

3. Earth has one moon, which is about 239,000 miles away. The surface of the moon is covered with millions of craters, flat areas called maria, and rocky areas called highlands. **TRUE FALSE**

4. The moon causes Earth's rotation to slow down by about two milliseconds every hundred years. **TRUE FALSE**

5. No one is sure how old Earth is, but some scientists think it was formed about 4 or 5 years ago. **TRUE FALSE**

6. A mixture of gases around Earth makes up the air, which we call the atmosphere. **TRUE FALSE**

7. These gases are primarily nitrogen, oxygen, and farts. **TRUE FALSE**

8. Some scientists believe that about 900 million years ago Earth had 481 eighteen-hour days in a year. **TRUE FALSE**

lets take over the world
can I have a bannana.
whats that smell?
can yeu tern into a yoneacorn.

Howling at the Moon

Q. What kind of ticks live on the moon?
A. Lunar-ticks!

Q. Why did Ricky's Mighty Robot climb up the Empire State Building?
A. Because he didn't fit in the elevator.

Q. What did Victor Von Vulture cook for lunch?
A. An unidentified frying object!

Q. How did Mr. Mosquito tie his shoes?
A. With astro-knots.

Q. What kind of fur do you get from a Jurassic Jackrabbit?
A. As fur away as possible.

Knock knock.
Who's there?
Athena.
Athena who?
Athena Thtupid Thtinkbug fly by!

Q. Why is Ricky Ricotta's Mighty Robot so
courageous?
A. Because he has nerves of steel.

Q. What steps should you take if a Uranium
Unicorn sneaks up behind you?
A. Really big ones.

Q. How do you make a Mecha-Monkey float?
A. Take two scoops of ice cream, then add some
soda, chocolate syrup, and a Mecha-Monkey.
Stir well.

Q. How did Sergeant Stinkbug
get clean?
A. He took a meteor shower.

Q. How do you stop a Stupid
Stinkbug from smelling?
A. Hold its nose.

HOW TO DRAW DR. STINKY McNASTY

1.

2.

3.

4.

5.

6.

7.

8.

9.

10.

11.

12.

Rocket Racer

Do you have a need for speed? Make your own Rocket Racer using the supplies below.

2 balloons
1 24-inch piece of yarn
1 plastic drinking straw
1 rubber band
Magic Markers

masking or Scotch tape
scissors
a Mighty Robot (or a tall human, like a grown-up)
a room with a ceiling

1. Blow up one balloon and tie the end in a knot. Then tie the yarn around the knot. Use markers to decorate the balloon to look like your favorite planet.

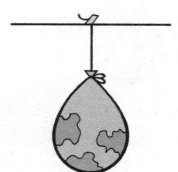

2. Ask your Mighty Robot to tape one end of the yarn to the ceiling.

3. Cut the plastic straw in half.

4. Carefully stick one inch of the straw into the opening of the second balloon.

5. Loop a rubber band around the area where the balloon covers the straw and continue to wrap the rubber band around and around until the straw is held in place.

6. Blow through the straw to inflate your balloon as big as you can without popping it. Then pinch the straw shut over the rubber band.

7. Aim your Rocket Racer for the planet hanging from the ceiling, and let go. Try to hit the planet for a super-space landing!

MARS

Major Monkey see!

Mecha-Monkeys do!

These Martian

monsters belong

in a zoo!

TRUE-OR-FALSE FACTS
Which facts are fake? Circle true or false.

1. Mars is the fourth planet from the sun. It is often called the Red Planet because it is covered with a layer of red dust. **TRUE FALSE**

2. This red dust has a delicious strawberry flavor. Just one spoonful, stirred into milk, provides eight vitamins and nutrients. **TRUE FALSE**

3. Mars is smaller than Earth but bigger than Mercury and Pluto.
TRUE FALSE

4. Usually the temperature on Mars is about 67 degrees below zero. But sometimes it is as cold as 200 degrees below zero and as warm as 80 degrees. **TRUE FALSE**

5. Mars has an ice cap on each of its poles but no seas or rivers. Liquid water doesn't exist there. It hasn't rained on Mars for about 3 billion years. **TRUE FALSE**

6. Mars has extremely violent storms. However, the sky is pink, so nobody takes the storms seriously. **TRUE FALSE**

7. Mars has two tiny moons. **TRUE FALSE**

8. The moon's names are Lisa and Steve.
TRUE FALSE

Monster Mash

These mangy monsters are dancing in the dark. Can you name them all? Next, find their shapes by shading in the pieces of the puzzle on the right.

1. m eeha- monkey

2. robo cimp

3. General jackrabbt

4. cupcake

5. mighty robot

6. uncle unicorn

7. victor von vulfury

8. _____

9. waffles

10. _____

11. major monkey

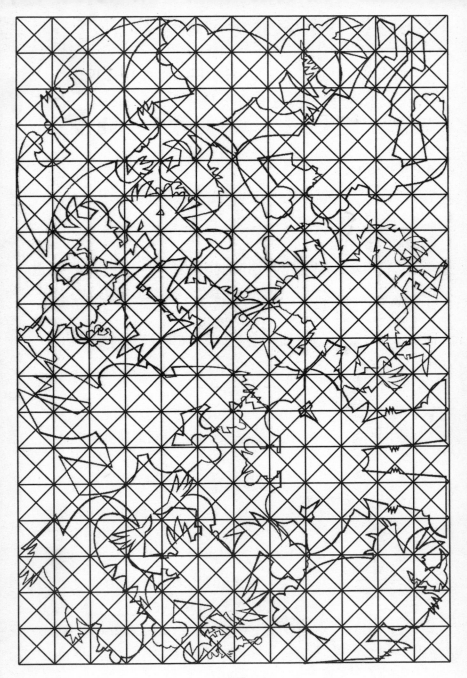

How well do you know the baddies in the Ricky Ricotta books? Use the clues to fill in the answers in the crossword puzzle on the right.

ACROSS

1. Dr. _____ McNasty invented the Mighty Robot.

2. _____ Monkey's laboratory turned into a giant Orangu-Tron.

4. Don't mess with the Un-Pleasant _____ from Pluto.

6. Lucy's _____ Jackrabbits are named Fudgie, Cupcake, and Waffles.

9. _____ Unicorn built a giant Ladybot to trick Ricky's Robot.

10. The _____ Vultures love to eat.

11. The _____ Night Crawlers are from Neptune.

12. The _____ -Chimps work for Major Monkey.

DOWN

1. The smelliest creatures in the galaxy are _____ Stinkbugs.

2. Mr. _____ doesn't want to live on Mercury.

3. Victor Von _____ used a voodoo remote controller to take over Squeakyville.

5. The _____ -Monkeys flew home to Mars.

7. _____ Jackrabbit landed his rocket ship on the roof of the museum.

8. Ricky's Mighty Robot fell in love with the _____ .

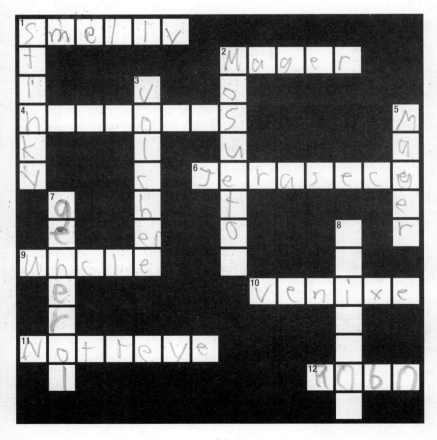

JUPITER

Jiggle, joggle,

juggle!

General Jackrabbit

gets a jot jumpy

on Jupiter!

TRUE-OR-FALSE FACTS
Which facts are fake? Circle true or false.

1. Jupiter is enormous, but it's mostly made of hydrogen and helium gas. If you travel below Jupiter's clouds, you won't find a solid surface. **TRUE FALSE**

2. Jupiter is the largest planet in our solar system. It if were a hollow ball, Jupiter could contain more than one thousand Earths. **TRUE FALSE**

3. Jupiter has at least 60 moons, including the biggest moon in our solar system, Ganymede, which is larger than Mercury. **TRUE FALSE**

4. Jupiter gets its orange-red color from its many carrot farms. Carrots are the chief export of Jupiter, followed by glazed donuts and Chinese finger traps. **TRUE FALSE**

5. Jupiter has extremely strong winds. They blow up to 400 miles per hour! **TRUE FALSE**

6. The largest storm on Jupiter is called the Great Red Spot, and it is bigger than two Earths. **TRUE FALSE**

7. Jupiter has the shortest day of any planet—less than 10 hours. **TRUE FALSE**

8. Jupiter has rings like Saturn, but they're hard to see. **TRUE FALSE**

9. Jupiter has a delightful cinnamon flavor. **TRUE FALSE**

Jupiter Jet

Make a super-speedy paper jet plane by following the steps below.

1. Start with a new piece of 8¹/₂ x 11-inch paper with no holes or tears.

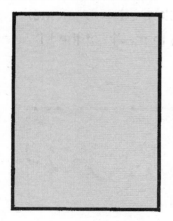

FOLD

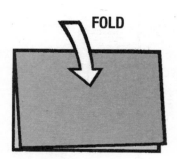

2. Fold it in half from top to bottom so that the edges line up.

3. Fold the bottom right corner of the top layer up so it lines up with the crease you made in step 2.

FOLD

4. Fold the bottom left corner of the top layer up so it lines up with the crease you made in step 2. The top layer will look like an upside-down triangle.

5. Fold the top right corner down to the tip of the triangle.

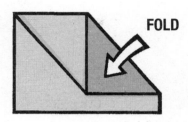

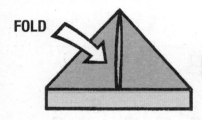

6. Fold the top left corner down to the tip of the triangle.

7. Unfold the last two folds you made. You will see two diagonal crease marks.

8. Fold the top right and top left corners down so they line up with the crease marks.

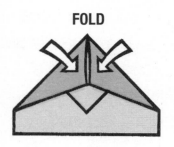

FOLD

9. Fold the top right and top left sides down along the same crease marks. The middle layer of paper will be a V-shaped flap.

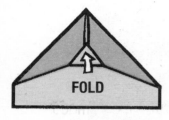

Turn over

FOLD

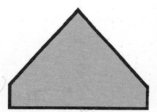

10. Fold the V-shaped flap up.

The side facing up should look like this.

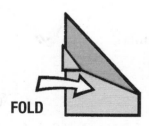

FOLD

11. Fold it in half from left to right so the edges line up.

12. Fold the top flap down along the line in the picture.

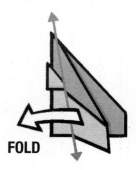

FOLD

13. You just made the first wing.

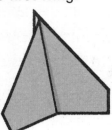

Turn over

The side facing up should look like this.

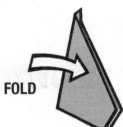

FOLD

14. Make the second wing by folding the paper from left to right so the smooth edges line up.

15. Gently unfold the wings so the plane looks like this from behind.

16. Make a small fold in each wing for the fins.

Your Jupiter Jet is ready for take-off!

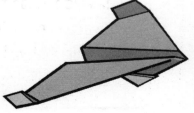

Planet Planner

Are there only nine planets in our solar system? Scientists don't know for sure, but they are always trying to learn more about the galaxy. Imagine that you have discovered a new planet, and share your findings below:

What is the name of your planet?

~~Saptune~~ Pooppo

What color is it?

light blue brown

What is it made of?

rocks, water, ice

Does it have rings or moons? How many?

it has twelve moons

What is the temperature?

L, 68 f, H, 82 f

✴ E X T R A - T E R R E S T R I A L   T I P ✴
Look back at the planets you've visited
so far for ideas.

EXTRA! EXTRA! EXTRA!

Sebtin **DISCOVERS** Plootoooe

(your name)   (your planet)

Pooopoo

(draw a picture of your planet above)

SATURN

Sergeant Stinkbug has such a bad smell—when he walks by, even the trash can tell!

TRUE-OR-FALSE FACTS
Which facts are fake? Circle true or false.

1. Like Jupiter, Saturn is mostly gas with a rocky core. But winds blow even harder than they do on Jupiter—around Saturn's equator, winds are more than ten times worse than a hurricane. **TRUE FALSE**

2. Saturn has more than 30 moons. One of them, called Titan, even has its own atmosphere. **TRUE FALSE**

3. Saturn's thousands of narrow rings are made up of sweet marshmallow surprises: pink hearts, yellow moons, orange stars, and green clovers. Many astronomers believe that these elements may be part of a nutritious breakfast. **TRUE FALSE**

4. Saturn was discovered in 1988 by a guy named Greg, who works at the gas station over by Wal-Mart. **TRUE FALSE**

5. Some of Saturn's moons are very strange. One moon, called Mimas, has a giant crater that makes it look like the Death Star from the Star Wars movies. Another, called Hyperion, is shaped like a garbage can. **TRUE FALSE**

6. One day on Saturn lasts about ten-and-a-half Earth hours. **TRUE FALSE**

7. Saturn is the second largest planet in our solar system. **TRUE FALSE**

Silly Stinky Sentences

These sentences are so silly that you read them from top to bottom.

S <u>OME</u>

A <u>NIMALS</u>

T <u>URN</u>

U GLY

R <u>EALLY</u>

N <u>ICELY</u>

Fill in each blank with a
word that starts with the
letter listed. Then read
your silly sentence.

S tinkbugs

T ry

I n

N uggets

K akrotch

B ug

U gly

G rose

S oup

EARTHLING EXAM

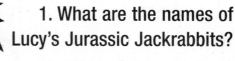

1. What are the names of Lucy's Jurassic Jackrabbits?

A. Itchy, Scratchy, and Runny.
B. Fudgie, Cupcake, and Waffles.
C. Spinach, Broccoli, and Lima Beans.

2. What did Ricky give the Voodoo Vultures to eat?

A. Pancakes filled with fresh blueberries.
B. Grilled cheese sandwiches filled with peanut butter.
C. Chocolate chip cookies filled with super red-hot chili peppers.

3. How does the Mighty Robot help Ricky's family?

A. He uses his super breath to blow leaves away.
B. He scares the neighbors so they won't come visit.
C. He opens the door so burglars can walk right in.

4. Which of these creatures do not come from Mars?

A. Robo-Chimps.
B. Orangu-Trons.
C. Banana-Bots.

Stinkbug´s Stomach Maze

Q. Which side of Saturn is always visible?
A. The outside.

Q. Which Un-Pleasant Penguins wear the biggest helmets?
A. The ones with the biggest heads.

Ricky: Did you hear the joke about the sun?
Lucy: nope.
Ricky: never mind—it's way over your head.

Q. What did Major Monkey do when Ricky's Robot stepped on his tail?
A. He went to a retail store.

Q. Why did Uncle Unicorn buy cough drops?
A. Because he was a little hoarse.

Q. What do space chipmunks eat?
A. Astro-nuts.

Q. How does the man in the moon cut his hair?
A. Eclipse it.

Q. What is Ricky's Mighty Robot's favorite snack?
A. Microchips.

Q. What time is it when five Voodoo Vultures are chasing you?
A. Time to run!

Q. What resembles half of a Naughty Night Crawler?
A. The other half.

Q. Why do Mutant Mosquitoes buzz?
A. Because they don't know the words.

Q. If a meteor that hits Earth is called a meteorite, what do you call one that misses?
A. A meteor-wrong.

Q. How did the Stupid Stinkbug call his friend?
A. On his smell phone.

Q. What do Mecha-Monkeys drink on the moon?
A. Crater-ade.

Stinkbug Shuffle

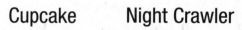

Try to find
the words
below in
the puzzle
on the right.
Look across, down,
diagonally, and backwards.

Cupcake	Night Crawler
Fudgie	Penguin
Jurassic	Ricky
Ladybot	Stinkbug
Lucy	Stinky McNasty
Major Monkey	Uranium
Mighty Robot	Victor
Mosquito	Waffles

> ✷ EARTHLING EXTRA ✷
> One of the words on page 20 is hidden in this puzzle.
> If you can find it, you're a word find whiz!

```
G U B K N I T S C V O O G Y H
A C U P C A K E B D E F Y E M
R P Z E F L A D Y B O T Q K I
E I V N R F U C R I S A B N T
M L C G Q O U C V A M Y L O O
Z V L U M L T M N L U C P M B
R I N I G H T C R A W L E R O
D C U N V O M I I M A Y N O R
O T R A B Y I S R V K W G J Y
O A A C K O K S Q C W A X A T
V L N N E F R A I Z O F L M H
F E I G D U F R E W A F F O G
N T U A F I T U S U W L E N I
S K M O S Q U J N F Q E F X M
L O O J R N O T I U Q S O M P
```

URANUS

Evil Uncle Unicorn has a twisted, jagged horn. He also has a nasty plot: build a giant Ladybot!

TRUE-OR-FALSE FACTS
Which facts are fake? Circle true or false.

1. Uranus was named after the Greek god of butts. **TRUE FALSE**

2. Uranus is about four times the size of Earth. It is covered by thick, blue-green clouds of methane gas. **TRUE FALSE**

3. Each year on Uranus lasts 84 Earth years (42 years of sunlight followed by 42 years of darkness). **TRUE FALSE**

4. Uranus has the funniest name of any planet, except for Planet Diarrhea. **TRUE FALSE**

5. Uranus has more than 20 moons.
TRUE FALSE

6. Uranus is very, very cold. It can get as nippy as 350 degrees below zero. **TRUE FALSE**

7. Uranus was originally named "George's Star." **TRUE FALSE**

8. Uranus was first discovered by a guy named Herschel. At first, he thought it was a comet.
TRUE FALSE

Runaway Ricky Maze

★RICKY RICOTTA'S★
MIGHTY ROBOT

MERCURY

MARS

EARTH

VENUS

PO # 227848

Published by the Blue Sky Press / Scholastic Inc. www.pilkey.com www.scholastic.com/rickyricotta S-TK1-82601-2.

JUPITER

NEPTUNE

URANUS

SATURN

PLUTO

PO • 227651

EXTRA EARTHLING EXAM

1. What is Lucy's favorite game to play?

A. Duck, duck, goose.
B. Princess.
C. Hide-and-seek.

2. How did Fudgie and Cupcake defeat the Ladybot?

A. They zapped her with a laser beam.
B. They stuck a sign saying "Kick me!" on her back.
C. They tied her shoelaces together.

3. Why does Mr. Mosquito hate Mercury?

A. Because it's full of Mecha-Monkeys.
B. Because it has hot days and cold nights.
C. Because it smells like bug spray.

4. What did Ricky eat while battling the Stupid Stinkbugs?

A. Grow-Big Gumballs.
B. Super-Sized Stinky-Snacks.
C. Robo-Powered Peanuts.

Who's Your Baddie?

As Ricky and his Robot know, every planet has a bad guy just waiting for his chance to take over Earth. Remember the planet you created on page 50? Describe the baddie living there.

What kind of animal is he?

cat

What is his name?

Kitty cat

What does he like?

pizza oo

What does he hate?

cat food

What kind of spaceship does he drive?

None

!!! WANTED !!!

If you have any information about this suspect, contact the Squeakyville Police Department.

that is not the planet I fond.

(draw a picture of your baddie above)

NEPTUNE

Neptune's Night Crawlers
are never nice.
Who wants to live
where it's colder
than ice?

TRUE-OR-FALSE FACTS
Which facts are fake? Circle true or false.

1. Winds on Neptune can blow more than 1,200 miles per hour. **TRUE FALSE**

2. Like Uranus, Neptune is about four times the size of Earth. **TRUE FALSE**

3. The blue color of the clouds surrounding Neptune is caused by the methane gas in its atmosphere. **TRUE FALSE**

4. Methane gas is a common ingredient found in farts. **TRUE FALSE**

5. Neptune is very, very cold. Frozen crystals of methane gas form white clouds that reach temperatures of 390 degrees below zero. **TRUE FALSE**

6. If you put your tongue on Neptune, it would probably get stuck there. **TRUE FALSE**

7. Neptune has seven moons. Their names are Dopey, Sleepy, Doc, Happy, Grumpy, Bashful, and Fabulous. **TRUE FALSE**

8. Neptune actually has rings like Saturn, but they're hard to see because Neptune is so bright. **TRUE FALSE**

9. Neptune was originally named "That Big Thingy Over There in the Sky." **TRUE FALSE**

★RICKY RICOTTA'S★
FILL-IN-THE-BLANK
ADVENTURE

Before you read the story on pages 74–81, go through and fill in all of the blanks.

Below each blank is a picture.

Find the matching picture on the opposite page.

Pick a word from the list below the matching picture.

Then write the word you picked in the blank.

now sit back and read your silly story with a friend.

ran
walked
flew
jumped
danced
swam

smelly
goofy
stupid
silly
crazy
purple

hamburger
toilet
kitty
frog
diaper
panty hose

sloppy
gross
disgusting
barf-covered
dripping
marshmallowy

scuba diver
school bus
walrus
monkey
chicken
accountant

Saturn
Stinkyville
Cleveland
Pluto
Planet Diarrhea
Uranus

RICKY RICOTTA'S MIGHTY ROBOT

VS. THE _Smelly_ , _Barf-covered_

CREATURE FROM _planet Diarrhea_

Written by _Corbin Eskridge_
(your name)

One _crazy_ morning, Ricky Ricotta and his

Mighty Robot decided to play a _sloppy_ game

of "Pin the _kitty_ on the _chicken_." So

they _ran_ to _planet diarrhea_ to play their

game. On the way, they heard a ~~dripping~~ noise.

Suddenly, an evil, _silly_ _kitty_ from

outer space _flew_ down from the sky.

Pick a word from the list below the matching picture. Then write the word you picked in the blank.

smashed
punched
kicked
kissed
licked
married

polka-dotted
yummy
wacky
furry
giant
hairy

armpits
butt
tongue
panty hose
nose
underwear

punching
kicking
kissing
licking
eating
marrying

rubber duckies
toasters
toilets
cupcakes
diapers
dirty socks

giraffes
elephants
camels
monkeys
sheep
poodles

"I have come to destroy all the toilets

on Earth," said the creature. Then he began

licking all of the dirty socks

and eating each of the toasters

with his furry tongue.

The Mighty Robot tried to stop the furry

monster by kicking him. But the evil creature

kicked Ricky's Robot on his butt.

"I've got a furry, hairy

idea," said Ricky. He ran to a store and bought

some exploding pootles.

disgusting
crunchy
dripping
slippery
funky
sweaty

ape's
monkey's
gorilla's
orangutan's
chimpanzee's
gym teacher's

gerbil
toilet
butt
hamster
stinky
potty

pickles
boogers
goobers
tofu
custard
bubbles

gigantic
powerful
incredible
horrible
creamy
chocolatey

armpits
flip-flops
underpants
diapers
tushie
girdle

78

Ricky hid the exploding animals in a _disgusting_ bowl of _butt boogers_. Then he gave it to the evil creature.

"Holy _underpants_," said the creature.

"This food smells worse than a big _gorilla's underpants_!"

But he was hungry, so he ate the _disgusting, horrible_ stuff anyway.

Suddenly, there was a _powerful_ explosion that was so _powerful_, it blew the creature's _tushie_ off.

punched
slapped
kicked
smacked
hammered
head-butted

face
nose
mouth
head
teeth
eyeballs

danced
swam
skipped
boogied
walked
wiggled

horrible
wimpy
terrible
stupid
crazy
goofy

punching
demolishing
fighting
destroying
battling
kissing

friends
pals
buddies
mutual acquaintances
monkeys
underpants

That _crazy_ monster just wouldn't give up. He tried _demolishing_ Ricky's Robot, but he missed. So Ricky's Mighty Robot _head-butt_ the _wimpy_ creature right on his _mouth_.

"I'm getting out of this _wimpy_ place," said the creature. So he picked up his _mouth_ and _walked_ back to his home planet.

"Thank you for working so _crazy_ together," said Ricky's father.

"No problem," said Ricky. "That's what _underpants_ are for!"

PLUTO

Puny, peewee
Pluto is an
un-pleasant place,
even for penguins
from outer space!

TRUE-OR-FALSE FACTS
Which facts are fake? Circle true or false.

1. Pluto is the smallest planet in our solar system, and much of the time it is the most distant planet from the sun. **TRUE FALSE**

2. Pluto is very cold. Its temperature ranges from about 350 degrees below zero at its warmest to 385 degrees below zero at its coldest. **TRUE FALSE**

3. The sunlight on Pluto is thought to be 1,500 times dimmer than sunlight on Earth.
TRUE FALSE

4. Nobody is sure what is inside Pluto. Its surface is believed to be made of paper mâché, while some speculate that its insides may contain a mixture of candy corn, gum, and fun-sized chocolate bars. **TRUE FALSE**

5. Pluto was named after Mickey Mouse's dog. **TRUE FALSE**

6. Pluto is more than 3.6 billion miles from the sun. If you rode a bike there at 5 miles an hour, it would take more than 82,000 years. **TRUE FALSE**

7. Recently, many scientists have argued about whether Pluto is really a planet, since other Pluto-like objects have also been detected in our solar system just past Neptune. These objects have orbits and properties similar to Pluto. **TRUE FALSE**

Cosmic Caper

Oh, no! It looks as if
Earth is under attack,
and only you and your
Robot can save the day!
Make up your own story,
using the questions on the
right to help you get started.

When you're done,
share your story
with a friend!

✳ EXTRA-TERRESTRIAL TIP ✳

For extra fun, you can use the robot you created
on page 24, the planet you created on page 50,
and the baddie you created on page 66.
You can also look at the silly story that starts on
page 75 for more ideas.

WHO are the characters?

_____

_____

_____

_____

WHERE does this story take place?

_____

_____

WHEN does it take place?

_____

_____

WHAT happens?

_____

_____

_____

_____

WHY do the characters act the way they do?

_____

_____

_____

_____

THE PUZZLE FROM

How well do you know Ricky Ricotta's adventures? Use the clues to fill in the answers in the crossword puzzle on the right.

ACROSS

2. Ricky traveled to _____ to save his Robot from Major Monkey.

6. General Jackrabbit jumped for joy when he left _____ .

7. All the bad guys in the solar system want to take over _____ .

8. Mercury is the planet closest to the _____ .

9. The Mutant Mosquitoes from _____ battled Ricky's Robot.

10. Dr. Stinky McNasty built the Mighty Robot in a secret _____ .

13. Beware the Naughty Night Crawlers from _____ .

14. The bullies chased Ricky on his way to _____ .

DOWN

1. _____ is a polluted planet full of stupid, smelly Stinkbugs.

3. Ricky Ricotta and his family live in _____ .

4. Ricky's Mighty Robot sleeps in the Ricotta family's _____ .

5. Watch out for the Uranium Unicorns from _____ !

11. Victor Von Vulture hates _____ because it's too hot.

12. The Un-Pleasant Penguins come from _____ .

The Name Game

Write the name of each character next to the matching letter. Then write the letter next to something that character might say.

A _____   (E) I used to have a secret cave.

B _____   (K) My planet is a smelly dump!

C _____   (L) I drink banana juice.

D _____   (K) I have a Meany Machiney.

E _____   (B) My best friend is mighty big.

F _____   (H) I hypnotized Squeakyville.

G _____   (J) I love to play princess!

H _____   (I) I am very un-pleasant.

I _____   (D) I hate Mercury!

J _____   (A) I skateboard on a minivan.

K _____   (G) I built the Ladybot.

L _____   (C) I'm nasty and naughty.

Hello again! We're back on Earth, and it's good to be home. We hope you enjoyed visiting all the planets with us. We'll see you in our next adventure!

MERCURY
(Pages 6-7)
1. True; 2. True; 3. True; 4. False; 5. True; 6. True; 7. True; 8. False

EVIL ESCAPE MAZE
(Page 8)

MUTANT MOSQUITO MUMBLE-JUMBLE
(Page 9)
MESSY MELTED MILK CHOCOLATE MAKES MOSQUITOES MAD!

FUN IN THE SUN
(Page 12)
1. True; 2. True; 3. False;
4. True; 5. False;
6. True; 7. True

VENUS
(Pages 16-17)
1. True; 2. True;
3. True; 4. True;
5. False; 6. False; 7. True; 8. True; 9. True

DANGER DECODER
(Page 19)
ZAP ALL THE CHEESE IN SQUEAKYVILLE WITH ULTRA-EVIL VOODOO RAYS SO WE CAN TAKE OVER EARTH!

VERBAL VORTEX
(Page 21)

EARTH
(Pages 26-27)
1. True; 2. True; 3. True;
4. True; 5. False; 6. True;
7. False; 8. True

MARS
(Pages 36-37)
1. True; 2. False; 3. True;
4. True; 5. True; 6. True;
7. True; 8. False

MONSTER MASH
(Pages 38-39)
1. Mecha-Monkey
2. Robo-Chimp
3. Mutant Mosquito
4. Trihareatops
   (or Jurassic Jackrabbit)
5. Ladybot
6. Uranium Unicorn
7. Voodoo Vulture
8. Evil Monster (or Lizard)
9. Rabbidactyl
   (or Jurassic Jackrabbit)
10. Bunnysaurus Rex
    (or Jurassic Jackrabbit)
11. Stupid Stinkbug

MONKEY BUSINESS
(Page 41)

	S	T	I	N	K	Y							
	T						M	A	J	O	R		
	U			V			O						
	P	E	N	G	U	I	N	S				M	
	I			L			S					E	
	D			T		J	U	R	A	S	S	I	C
	G			U			I			L		H	
	E			R			T		L		A	
U	N	C	L	E			O		A			
	E						V	O	O	D	O	O
	R								Y		B	
N	A	U	G	H	T	Y						
	L								R	O	B	O

JUPITER
(Pages 44-45)
1. True; 2. True;
3. True; 4. False;
5. True; 6. True;
7. True; 8. True;
9. False

SATURN
(Pages 52-53)
1. True; 2. True;
3. False; 4. False;
5. True; 6. True;
7. True

EARTHLING EXAM
(Page 56)
1. B; 2. C; 3. A; 4. C

STINKBUG'S
STOMACH MAZE
(Page 57)

START   FINISH

93

STINKBUG SHUFFLE
(Page 61)
The extra word from page 20 is Squeakyville.

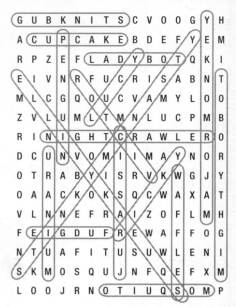

URANUS
(Pages 62-63)
1. False; 2. True; 3. True;
4. True AND False: Planet
Diarrhea is not a real planet,
but Uranus still has the
funniest name; 5. True;
6. True; 7. True; 8. True

RUNAWAY RICKY
MAZE
(Page 64)

EXTRA EARTHLING EXAM
(Page 65)
1. B; 2. C; 3. B; 4. A

NEPTUNE
(Pages 70-71)
1. True; 2. True; 3. True; 4. True; 5. True; 6. True; 7. False;
8. True; 9. False

PLUTO
(Pages 82-83)
1. True; 2. True; 3. True;
4. False; 5. False;
6. True; 7. True

THE PUZZLE FROM
ANOTHER PLANET
(Page 87)

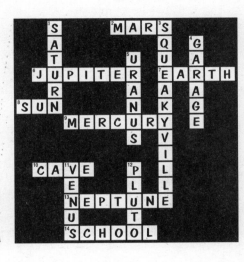

THE NAME GAME
(Page 89)
A. Mighty Robot; B. Ricky Ricotta; C. Victor Von Vulture
(or Voodoo Vulture); D. Mr. Mosquito; E. Dr. Stinky McNasty;
F. Sergeant Stinkbug (or Stupid Stinkbug); G. Uncle Unicorn
(or Uranium Unicorn); H. General Jackrabbit; I. Un-Pleasant Penguin;
J. Lucy; K. Naughty Night Crawler; L. Major Monkey

Sentence Answers (from top to bottom): E, F, L, H, B, C, J, I, D, A, G, K

DON'T MISS RICKY'S OTHER ADVENTURES:

Ricky Ricotta's Mighty Robot

AND

RICKY RICOTTA'S MIGHTY ROBOT

VS.

The Mutant Mosquitoes from Mercury

The Voodoo Vultures from Venus

The Mecha-Monkeys from Mars

The Jurassic Jackrabbits from Jupiter

The Stupid Stinkbugs from Saturn

The Uranium Unicorns from Uranus

The Naughty Night Crawlers from Neptune

The Un-Pleasant Penguins from Pluto